THE WAKER DREAMS

THE WAKER DREAMS

by Richard Matheson

If one flew over the city at this time of this day, which was like any other day in the year 3850, one would think all life had disappeared.

Sweeping over the rustless spires, one would search in vain for the sight of human activity. One's gaze would scan the great ribboned highways that swept over and under each other like the weave of some tremendous loom. But there would be no autocars to see; nothing but the empty lanes and the colored traffic lights clicking out their mindless progressions.

Dipping low and weaving in and out among the glittering towers, one might see the moving walks, the studied revolution of the giant street ventilators, hot in the winter and cool in summer, the tiny doors opening and closing, the park fountains shooting their methodical columns of water into the air.

Farther along, one would flit across the great open field on which the glossy spaceships stood lined before their hangars. Farther yet, one would catch sight of the river, the metal ships resting along shore, delicate froth streaming from their sterns caused by the never-ending operation of their vents.

Again, one would glide over the city proper, seeking some sign of life in the broad avenues, the network of streets, the painstaking pattern of dwellings in the living area, the metal fastness of the commercial section.

The search would be fruitless.

All movement below would be seen to be mechanical. And, knowing what city this was, one's eyes would stop the search for citizens and seek out those squat metal structures which stood a half mile apart. These circular buildings housed the never-resting machines, the humming geared servants of the city's people.

These were the machines that did all; cleared the air of impurities, moved the walks and opened the doors, sent their synchronized impulses into the traffic lights, operated the fountains and the spaceships, the river vessels and the ventilators.

THE WAKER DREAMS

These were the machines in whose flawless efficacy the people of the city placed their casual faith.

At the moment, these people were resting on their pneumatic couches in rooms. And the music that seeped from their wall speakers, the cool breezes that flowed from their wall ventilators, the very air they breathed—all these were of and from the machines, the unfailing, the trusted, the infallible machines.

Now there was a buzzing in ears. Now the city came alive.

*

There was a buzzing, buzzing. From the black swirl of slumber, you heard it. You wrinkled up your classic nose and twitched the twenty neural rods that led to the highways of your extremities.

The sound bore deeper, cut through swaths of snooze and poked an impatient finger in the throbbing matter of your brain. You twisted your head on the pillow and grimaced.

There was no cessation. With stupored hand, you reached out and picked up the receiver. One eye propped open by dint of will, you breathed a weary mutter into the mouthpiece.

"Captain Rackley!" The knifing voice put your teeth on edge.

"Yes," you said.

"You will report to your company headquarters immediately!"

That swept away sleep and annoyance as a petulant old man brushes chessmen from his board. Stomach muscles drew into play and you were sitting. Inside your noble chest, that throbbing meat ball, source of blood velocity, saw fit to swell and depress with marked emphasis. Your sweat glands engaged in proper activity, ready for action, danger, heroism.

"Is it...?" you started.

"Report immediately!" the voice crackled, and there was a severe click in your ear.

You, Justin Rackley, dropped the receiver—plunko—in its cradle and leaped from bed in a shower of fluttering bedclothes.

RICHARD MATHESON

You raced to your wardrobe door and flung it open. Plunging into the depths, you soon emerged with your skintight pants, the tunic for your forty-two chest. You donned said trousers and tunic, flopped upon a nearby seat and plunged your arches into black military boots.

*

And your face reflected oh-so-grim thoughts. Combing out your thick blond hair, you were sure you knew what the emergency was.

The Rustons! They were at it again!

Awake now, you wrinkled your nose with conscious aplomb. The Rustons made revolting food for thought with their twelve legs, sign of alien progenitors, and their exudation of foul reptilian slime.

As you scurried from your room, leaped across the balustrade and down the stairs, you wondered once again where these awful Rustons had originated, what odious interbreeding produced their monster race. You wondered where they lived, where proliferated their grisly stock, held their meetings of war, began the upward slither to those great Earth fissures from which they massed in attack.

With nothing approaching answers to these endless questions, you ran out of the dwelling and flew down the steps to your faithful autocar. Sliding in, pushing buttons, levers, pedals, what have you, you soon had it darting through the streets toward the broad highway that led to headquarters.

At this time of day, naturally, there were very few people about. In point of fact you saw none. It was only a few minutes later, when you turned sharply and zoomed up the ramp to the highway, that you saw the other autocars whizzing toward the tower five miles distant. You guessed, and were correct in guessing, that they were fellow officers, all similarly ripped from slumber by mobilization.

Buildings flew past as you pushed pedals deeper into their cavities, your face always grim, alive to danger, grand warrior! True, you were not averse to the chance for activity after a month of idleness. But the circumstances *were* slightly distasteful. To think of the Rustons made a fellow shudder, eh?

THE WAKER DREAMS

What made them pour from their unknown pits? Why did they seek to destroy the machines, let the acid canker of their ooze eat through metal, make the teeth fall off the gears like petals off a dying flower? What was their purpose? Did they mean to ruin the city? Govern its inhabitants? Or slaughter them? Ugly questions, questions without answers.

Well, you thought as you drove into headquarters parking area, thank heaven the Rustons had only managed to get at a few of the outer machines, yours blessedly not included.

They, at least, had no more idea than you where the Great Machine was, that fabulous fountainhead of energy, driver of all machines.

You slid the seat of your military trousers across the seat of the autocar and jumped out into the wide lot. Your black boots clacked as you ran toward the entrance. Other officers were getting out of autocars, too, running across the area. None of them said anything; they all looked grim. Some of them nodded curtly at you as you all stood together in the rising elevator. Bad business, you thought.

With a tug at the groin, the door gave a hydraulic gasp and opened. You stepped out and padded silently down the hall to the high-ceilinged briefing room.

Already the room was almost filled. The young men, invariably handsome and muscular, stood in gregarious formations, discussing the Rustons in low voices. The gray soundproof walls sucked in their comments and returned dead air.

*

The men gave you a look and a nod when you entered, then returned to their talking. Justin Rackley, captain, that's you, sat down in a front seat.

Then you looked up. The door to Upper Echelons was jerked open. The General came striding through, a sheaf of papers in his square fist. *His* face was grim too.

He stepped up on the rostrum and slapped the papers on the thick table which stood there. Then he plumped down on the edge of it and kicked his boot against one of its legs until all your fellow officers had broken up their groups and hurriedly taken seats. With silence creeping over all heads, he pursed his lips and banged a palm on the table surface.

"Gentlemen," he said with that voice which seemed to issue from an ancient tomb, "once more the city lies in grave danger."

He then paused and looked capable of handling all emergencies. You hoped that someday you might be General and look capable of handling all emergencies. No reason why not, you thought.

"I will not take up precious time," the General went on, taking up precious time. "You all know your positions, you all know your responsibilities. When this briefing is concluded, you will report to the arsenal and draw out your ray guns. Always remember that the Rustons must not be allowed to enter the machinery and live. Shoot to kill. The rays are *not* harmful, repeat, *not* harmful to the machinery."

He looked over you eager young men.

"You also know," he said, "the dangers of Ruston poisoning. For this reason, that the slightest touch of their stingers can lead to abysmal agonies of death, you will be assigned, as you also know, a nurse trained in the combating of systemic poisons. Therefore, after leaving the arsenal, you will report to the Preventive Section."

He winked, a thoroughly out-of-place wink.

"And remember," he said, with a broad roll of import in his voice, "this is *war*! And *only* war!"

This, of course, brought on appreciative smiles, a smattering of leers and many unmilitary asides. Upon which the General snapped out of his brief role as chuckling confrere and returned to strict autocratic detachment.

"Once assigned a nurse, those of you whose machines are more than fifteen miles from the city will report to the spaceport, there to be assigned a spacecar. All of you will then proceed with utmost dispatch. Questions?"

No questions.

"I need hardly remind you," completed the General, "of the importance of this defense. As you are well aware, should the Rustons penetrate our city, spread their ravaging to the core of our machine system, should they—heaven forfend!—locate the Great Machine, we may then expect nothing but the most merciless of butchery. The city would be undone, we would all be annihilated, Man would be overthrown."

*

The men looked at him with clenched fists, patriotism lurching through their brains like drunken satyrs, yours included, Justin Rackley.

"That is all," said the General, waving his hand. "Good shooting."

He jumped down from the platform and swept through the doorway, the door opening magically a split second before his imperious nose stood to shatter on its surface.

You stood up, muscles tingling. Onward! Save our fair city!

You stepped through the broken ranks. The elevator again, standing shoulder to shoulder with your comrades, a fluttering sense of hyper-awareness coursing your healthy young body.

The arsenal room. Sound lost in the heavily padded interior. You, on line, grim-faced always, shuffling along, weapon bound. A counter; it was like an exchange market. You showed the man your identity card and he handed you a shiny ray gun and a shoulder case of extra ray pellets.

Then you passed through the door and scuffed down the rubberized steps to the Preventive Section. Corpuscles took a carnival ride through your veins.

You were fourth in line and she was fourth in line; that's how she was assigned to you.

You perused her contours, noting that her uniform, although similar to yours, somehow hung differently on her. This sidetracked martial contemplations for the nonce. *Zowie hoopla*—your libido clapped its calloused hands.

"Captain Rackley," said the man, "this is Miss Lieutenant Forbes. She is your only guarantee against death should you be stung by a Ruston. See that she remains close by at all times."

This seemed hardly an onerous commission and you saluted the man. You then exchanged a flicker of lids with the young lady and intoned a gruff command, relative to departure. This roused the two of you to walk to the elevator.

Riding down in silence, you cast glances at her. Long forgotten threnodies twitched into life in your revitalized brain. You were much taken by the dark ringlets that hung over her forehead and massed on her shoulders like curled black fingers. Her eyes, you noted, were brown and soft as eyes in a dream. And why shouldn't they be?

Yet something lacked. Some retardation kept bringing you down from ethereal cogitation. Could it, you wondered, be duty? And, remembering what you were out to do, you suddenly feared again. The pink clouds marched away in military formation.

Miss Lieutenant Forbes remained silent until the spacecar which you were assigned was flitting across the sky beyond the outskirts of the city. Then, following your somewhat banal overtures regarding the weather, she smiled her pretty little smile and showed her pretty little dimples.

"I am but sixteen," she announced.

"Then this is your first time."

"Yes," she replied, gazing afar. "I am very frightened."

You nodded, you patted her knee with what you meant to be a parental manner, but which, post-haste, brought the crimson of modesty flaming into her cheeks.

"Just stay close to me," you said, trying hard for a double meaning. "I'll take care of you."

THE WAKER DREAMS

Primitive, but good enough for sixteen. She blushed more deeply.

The city towers flashed beneath. Far off, like a minute button on the fringes of spiderweb, you saw your machine. You eased the wheel forward; the tiny ship dipped down and began a long glide toward Earth. You kept your eyes on the control board with strict attention, wondering about this strange sense of excitement running pell mell through your body, not knowing whether it presaged combat fatigue of one sort or another.

This was war. The city first. Hola!

*

The ship floated down to and hovered over the machine as you threw on the air brakes. Slowly, it sank to the roof like a butterfly settling on a flower.

You threw off the switch, heart pounding, all forgotten but the present danger. Grabbing the ray gun, you jumped out and ran to the edge of the roof.

Your machine was beyond the perimeter of the city. There were fields about. Your keen eyes flashed over the ground.

There was no sign of the enemy.

You hurried back to the ship. She was still sitting inside watching you. You turned the knob and the communicator system spilled out its endless drones of information. You stood impatiently until the announcer spoke your machine number and said the Rustons were within a mile of it.

You heard her drawn-in breath and noted the upward cast of frightened eyes in your direction. You turned off the set.

"Come, we'll go inside," you said, holding the ray gun in a delightfully shaking hand. It was fun to be frightened. A fine sense of living dangerously. Wasn't that why you were here?

You helped her out. Her hand was cold. You squeezed it and gave her a half smile of confidence. Then, locking the door to the spacecar, to keep the foe out, you took her arm and the two of you went down the stairs. As you entered the main room, your head was at once filled with the smooth hum of machinery.

Here, at this juncture of the adventure, you put down your ray gun and ammunition and explained the machinery to her. It is to be noted that you had no particular concern for the machinery as you spoke, being more aware of her proximity. Such charm, such youth, crying out for comfort.

You soon held her hand again. Then you had your arm around her lithesome waist and she was close. Something other than military defense planned itself in your mind.

Came the moment when she flicked up her drowsy lids and looked you smack-dab in the eye, as is the archaic literary passage. You found her violet eyes somewhat unbalancing. You drew her closer. The perfume of her rosy breath tied casual knots in your limbs. And yet there was still something holding you back.

Swish! Slap!

She stiffened and cried out.

The Rustons were at the walls!

*

You raced for the table upon which your ray gun rested. On the couch next to the table was your ammunition. You slung the case over your shoulder. She ran up to you and, sternly, you handed her the preventive case. You felt like the self-assured General when he was in a grim mood.

"Keep the needles loaded and handy," you said. "I may...."

The sentence died as another great slobbering Ruston slapped against the wall. The sound of its huge suckers slurped on the outside. They were searching for the machinery in the basement.

You checked the gun. It was ready.

"Stay here," you muttered. "I have to go down."

You didn't hear what she said. You dashed down the stairs and came bouncing out into the basement just as the first horror gushed over the edge of a window onto its metal floor like a stream of gravity-defying lava.

*

The row of blinking yellow eyes turned on you; your flesh crawled. The great brown-gold monstrosity began to scuttle across toward the machines with an oily squish. You almost froze in fear.

Then instinct came to the fore. You raised the gun quickly. A crackling brilliantine blue ray leaped from the muzzle, touched the scaly body and enveloped it. Screeching and the smell of frying oil filled the air. When the ray had dissipated, the dead Ruston lay black and smoking on the floor, its slime running across the welded seams.

You heard the sound of suckers behind. You whirled, blasted the second of the Rustons into greasy oblivion. Still another slid over the window edge and started toward you. Another burst from the gun and another scorched hulk lay twitching on the metal.

You swallowed a great lump of excitement in your throat, your head snapping around, your body leaping from side to side. In a second, two more of them were moving toward you. Two bursts of ray; one missed. The second monster was almost upon you before you burst it into flaming chunks as it reared up to plunge its black stingers in your chest.

You turned quickly, cried out in horror.

One Ruston was just slipping down the stairs, another swishing toward you, the long stingers aimed at your heart. You pressed the button. A scream caught in your throat.

You were out of pellets!

You leaped to the side and the Ruston fell forward. You tore open the case and fumbled with the pellets. One fell and shattered uselessly on the metal. Your hands were ice, they shook terribly. The blood pounded through your veins, your hair stood on end. You felt scared and amused.

The Ruston lunged again as you slid the pellet into the ray gun. You dodged again—not enough! The end of one stinger slashed through your tunic, laid open your arm. You felt the burning poison shoot into your system.

You pressed the button and the monster disappeared in a cloud of unguent smoke. The basement machinery was secure against attack—the Rustons had bypassed it.

You leaped for the stairway. You had to save the machines, save her, save yourself!

Your boots banged up the metal chairs. You lunged into the great room of machines and swept a glance around.

A gasp tore open your mouth. She was collapsed on a couch, sprawled, inert. A Ruston line of slime ran down the front of her swelling tunic.

You whirled and, as you did, the Ruston vanished into the machinery, pushing its scaly body through the gear spaces. The slime dropped from its body and watery jaws. The machine stopped, started again, the racked wheels groaning.

*

The city! You leaped to the machine's edge and shot a blast from the ray gun into it. The brilliantine blue ray licked out, missed the Ruston. You fired again. The Ruston moved too fast, hid behind the wheels. You ran around the machine, kept on firing.

You glanced at her. How long did the poison take? They never said. Already in your flesh, however, the burning had begun. You felt as if you were going up in flames, as if great pieces of your body were about to fall off.

You had to get an injection for yourself and her.

Still the Ruston eluded you. You had to stop and put another pellet in the gun. The interior began to whirl around you; you were overpoweringly dizzy. You pressed the button again and again. The ray darted into the machine.

You reeled around with a sob and tore open your collar. You could hardly breathe. The smell of the singed suet, of the rays, filled your head. You stumbled around the machine, shot out another ray at the fast-moving Ruston.

Then, finally, when you were about to keel over, you got a good target. You pressed the button, the Ruston was enveloped in flame, fell in molten bits beneath the machine, was swallowed up by the waste exhaust.

You dropped the ray gun and staggered over to her.

The hypodermics were on the table.

You tore open her tunic and jabbed a needle into her soft white shoulder, shudderingly injected the antidote into her veins. You stuck another into your own shoulder, felt the sudden coolness run through your flesh and your bloodstream.

You sank down beside her, breathing heavily and closing your eyes. The violence of activity had exhausted you. You felt as though you would have to rest a month after this. And, of course, you would.

She groaned. You opened your eyes and looked at her. Your heavy breathing began again, but this time you knew where the excitement was coming from. You kept looking at her. A warm heat lapped at your limbs, caressed your heart. Her eyes were on you.

"I...." you said.

Then all holding back was ended, all doubt undone. The city, the Rustons, the machines—the danger was over and forgotten. She ran a caressing hand over your cheek.

*

"And when next you opened your eyes," finished the doctor, "you were back in this room."

Rackley laughed, his head quivering on the pillow, his hands twitching in glee.

"But my dear doctor," he laughed, "how fantastically clever of you to know everything. However do you do it, naughty man?"

The doctor looked down at the tall handsome man who lay on the bed, still shaking with breathless laughter.

"You forget," he said, "I inject you. Quite natural that I should know what happens then."

"Oh, quite! Quite!" cried Justin Rackley. "Oh, it was utterly, utterly fantastic. Imagine me!" He ran strong fingers over the swelling biceps of his arm. "*Me*, a hero!"

He clapped his hands together and deep laughter rumbled in his chest, his white teeth flashed against the glowing tan of his face. The sheet slipped, revealing the broad suppleness of his chest, the tightly ridged stomach muscles.

"Oh, dear me," he sighed. "Dear me, what *would* this dull existence be without your blessed injections to ease our endless boredom?"

The doctor looked coldly at him, his strong white fingers tightening into a bloodless fist. The thought plunged a cruel knife into his brain—this is the end of our race, the sorry peak of Man's evolution. This is the final corruption.

Rackley yawned and stretched his arms. "I must rest." He peered up at the doctor. "It was such a *fatiguing* dream."

He began to giggle, his great blond head lolling on the pillow. His hands striking at the sheet as though he would die of amusement.

"Do tell me," he gasped, "what on earth have you in those utterly delightful injections? I've asked you so often."

The doctor picked up his plastic bag. "Merely a combination of chemicals designed to exacerbate the adrenals on one hand and, on the other, to inhibit the higher brain centers. In short," he finished, "a potpourri of intensification and reduction."

"Oh, you always say that," said Justin Rackley. "But it *is* delightful. Utterly, charmingly delightful. You will be back in a month for my next dream and my dream playback?"

The doctor blew out a weary gust of breath. "Yes," he said, making no effort to veil his disgust. "I'll be back next month."

"Thank heavens," said Rackley, "I'm done with that awful Ruston dream for another five months. Ugh! It's so frightfully vile! I like the pleasanter dreams about mining and transporting ores from Mars and the Moon, and the adventures in food centers. They're so much nicer. But...." His lips twitched. "*Do* have more of those pretty young girls in them."

His strong, weary body twisted in delight.

"Oh, *do*," he murmured, his eyes shutting.

He sighed and turned slowly and exhaustedly onto his broad, muscular side.

*

The doctor walked through the deserted streets, his face tight with the old frustration. Why? Why? His mind kept repeating the word.

Why must we continue to sustain life in the cities? For what purpose? Why do we not let civilization in its last outpost die as it means to die? Why struggle to keep such men alive?

Hundreds, thousands of Justin Rackleys—well kept animals, mechanically bred and fed and massaged into fair and handsome form. Mechanically restrained, too, from physically turning into the fat white slugs that, mentally, they already were and would bodily resemble if left untended. Or die.

Why not let them? Why visit them every month, fill their veins with hypnotic drugs and sit back and watch them, one by one, go bursting into their dream worlds to escape boredom? Must he endlessly send his suggestions into their loosened brainways, fly them to planets and moons, crowd all forms of love and grand adventure into their mock-heroic dreams?

The doctor slumped tiredly and went into another dorm-building. More figures, strongly or beautifully made, passive on couches. More dream injections.

He made them, watched the figures stand and stumble to the wardrobes. Explorers' outfits this time, pith helmets and attractive shorts, snake boots and bared limbs. He stood at the window, saw them clamber into their autocars and drive away. He sat back and waited for them to return, knowing every move they would make, because he made them in his mind.

They would go out to the hydroponics tanks and fight off an invasion of Energy Eaters. Bigger than the Rustons and made of pure force, they threatened to suck the sustenance from the plants in the growing trays, the living, formless meat swelling immortally in the nutrient solutions. The Energy Eaters would be beaten off, of course. They always were.

Naturally. They were only dreams. Creatures of fantastic illusion, conjured in eager dreaming minds by chemical magic and dreary scientific incantation.

But what would all these Justin Rackleys say, these handsome and hopeless ruins of torpid flesh, if they found out how they were being fooled?

Found out that the Rustons were only mental fictions for objectifying simple rust and wear and converting them into fanciful monsters. Monsters which alone could feebly arouse the dim instinct for self-preservation which just barely existed in this lost race. Energy Eaters—beetles and spores and exhausted growth solutions. Mine Borers—vaporous beasties that had to be blasted out of the Lunar and Martian metal deposits. And others, still others, all of them threats to that which runs and feeds and renews a city.

And what would they say, these Justin Rackleys, upon the discovery that each of them, in their "dreams," had done genuine manual work? That their ray guns were spray guns or grease guns or air hammers, their death rays no more than streams of lubrication for rusting machines or insecticides or liquid fertilizer?

What would they say if they found out how they were tricked into breeding with aphrodisiacs in the guise of anti-poison shots? How they, with no healthy interest in procreation, were drugged into the furtherance of their spineless strain, a strain whose only function was to sustain the life-giving machines.

*

In a month he would return to Justin Rackley, *Captain* Justin Rackley. A month for rest, these people were so devoid of energy. It took a month to build up even enough strength to endure an injection of hypnotics, to oil a machine or tend a tray, and to bring forth one puny cell of life.

All for the machines, the city, for man....

The doctor spat on the immaculate floor of the room with the pneumatic couches.

The people were the machines, more than the machines themselves. A slave race, a detestable residue, hopeless, without hope.

Oh, how they would wail and swoon, he thought, getting grim pleasure in the notion, were they allowed to walk through that vast subterranean tunnel to the giant chamber where the Great Machine stood, that supposed source of all energy, and saw why they had to be tricked into working. The Great Machine had been designed to eliminate all human labor, tending the minor machines, the food plants, the mining.

But some wise one on the Control Council, centuries before, had had the wit to smash the Great Machine's mechanical brain. And now the Justin Rackleys would have to see, with their own unbelieving eyes, the rust, the rot, the giant twisted death of it.... But they wouldn't.

Their job was to dream of adventurous work, and work while dreaming.

For how long?